Home at Last

written by **Susan Middleton Elya**

illustrated by **Felipe Davalos**

LEE & LOW BOOKS Inc.

New York

Manufactured in China by South China Printing Co.

Book design by Christy Hale   Book production by The Kids at Our House

The text is set in Esprit
The illustrations are rendered in oil

(HC) 10   9   8   7   6   5   4   3
(PB) 10   9   8   7   6   5   4   3   2   1
First Edition

Library of Congress Cataloging-in-Publication Data
Elya, Susan Middleton.
Home at last / written by Susan Middleton Elya ; illustrated by Felipe Davalos.— 1st ed.
p. cm.
Summary: When she and her family move from Mexico to the United States,
eight-year-old Ana helps her mother adjust to the new situation by encouraging
her to learn English.
ISBN 1-58430-020-5 (hardcover)   ISBN 1-58430-272-0 (paperback)
1. Mexican Americans—Juvenile fiction. [1. Mexican Americans—Fiction.]
I. Davalos, Felipe, ill. II. Title.
PZ7.E562 Ho 2002   [E]—dc   212001029402

ISBN-13: 978-1-58430-020-5 (hardcover)   ISBN-13: 978-1-58430-272-8 (paperback)

To students learning English as a second language,
and to their teachers—S.M.E.

To all immigrant mothers—F.D.

Ana Patiño's family came to the United States when she was eight and her twin brothers, Jesús and Julio, were babies. They moved to a town surrounded by corn, and Papá took a job with Uncle Luis at the canning factory.

Papá and Mamá found an apartment on the third floor of a building. When they first arrived, Ana eagerly ran up the flights of stairs and looked out the window. The farm fields and big round trees were different from those in her village in Mexico. When Mamá looked out and sighed, Ana knew she was already missing home.

After the family settled in, Papá enrolled Ana in school. All the children spoke English except for a boy from Honduras. Ana's teacher asked the class to say hello to their new classmate. Ana was too shy to speak in the morning, but by afternoon she was saying hello back.

That night Papá asked, "¿Te gusta la escuela?" Do you like school?

"Sí," said Ana. "Me gusta." Yes, I like it.

Her parents smiled.

Mamá made supper while Papá told them about his new job. Papá had to start with sweeping and cleanup work, unlike Uncle Luis, who had been at the factory longer and could run a machine.

The next day Ana learned to say her name in English. Everyone in the class practiced with her. By the end of the day she had said "My name is Ana Patiño" a dozen times.

"¿Te gusta la maestra?" Papá asked that evening. Do you like your teacher?

"Sí, me gusta," said Ana. "Se llama señorita Silvers." Her name is Miss Silvers.

Ana played with the babies while Mamá boiled rice and beans. She knew Mamá missed all the relatives coming and going, eager to help with the twins.

Ana and Papá practiced their English together each night at supper. Mamá wanted to understand. "¿Qué dijeron?" she asked. What did you say?

"You could learn English too," Ana suggested.

"¡Inglés!" Mamá said. "¡Imposible!"

As the days passed, Mamá pointed out how nothing was the same as back home. At the grocery store things were in odd-looking packages with strange words. None of the clerks spoke Spanish.

Ana helped her mother pay at the register. One day the clerk forgot that there was a special sale on chicken and overcharged them. Mamá tried to argue about the price, but she could only say the words in Spanish.

"Speak English, lady!" the clerk snapped.

Ana tried to help explain, but the clerk was too busy. He shooed her away like he would a bird in the park. Mamá needed the chicken and had to pay the higher price.

They went to a different market the next time, but with having to carry Julio, Jesús, and the groceries on the bus, it was too hard. They ended up back at the store near the apartment. Mamá's smile would disappear every time she went in the doorway.

One day Miss Silvers gave Ana a note to take home. It was written in English in fancy handwriting. Ana couldn't read the cursive style, and Mamá couldn't read the English. Ana knew her mother was worried as she trudged up the stairs with the babies.

"¡Tantos escalones!" Mamá said. So many steps!

That evening Papá read the note: "Ana learns well." Then he repeated it in Spanish for Mamá. "Ana aprende bien."

Mamá looked relieved. She went back to her mending, shaking her head because Ana's dresses had gotten too short and there was no more hem to let down.

"Mamá should learn English," Ana said. Papá nodded his head. But they both knew how difficult it was for her to start over in America.

A few nights later Papá didn't come home on time. Mamá paced the floor with Jesús. He was running a fever, and Mamá wanted to get him some medicine.

"¿Dónde está tu papá?" Mamá asked Ana. Where is your father?

Seeing her brother cry, even Ana began to worry.

Mamá took Jesús and started knocking on the neighbors' doors for help. A man came into the hall, but he didn't understand her frantic Spanish.

"I don't understand what you're saying," he said before disappearing inside his apartment.

Just then Papá came up the stairs carrying some yellow fabric for Ana's new dress. He took the baby from Mamá's tired arms. "Vámonos a casa," he said. Let's go home.

Mamá got excited. "¿A México?"

"No," he said gently. "Al apartamento." To the apartment.

Papá went for medicine, and Ana helped give Jesús a sponge bath to bring down his fever. Mamá's hands were steady now that she had Papá to help her.

"¿Ahora aprenderás inglés?" Ana asked. Will you learn English now?

Mamá slowly nodded her head. "Okay."

Papá found an evening English class in the next town. He borrowed Uncle Luis' car, and they all rode there together.

Mamá chose a seat in the back of the classroom. With its high ceiling and green walls, the room was nothing like Ana's friendly looking school. The bare windows looked like a row of open mouths in the growing darkness.

Papá and Ana waved good-bye and took the babies home. They made supper as best they could. The whole time Ana wondered how Mamá was doing. Was anyone saying hello to her? Was the teacher friendly?

They returned at the end of class with some overcooked pork wrapped in a tortilla. Mamá ate it politely while they waited.

"¿Te gusta el maestro?" Ana asked. Do you like your teacher?

"Sí, me gusta," Mamá answered.

Mamá learned something new at every class—how to count, how to answer the phone, how to shop at the store.

Four weeks later Ana helped Mamá prepare for the first test, an oral exam. Mamá practiced speaking until she could answer each of Ana's questions quickly.

The night of the test Mamá sat silently during the drive to class. Ana knew she was worried. How she wished she could take the test for Mamá! Instead, Ana wished her mother good luck. "¡Buena suerte!"

When the family returned to pick Mamá up after class, she was waiting outside, her brown eyes sparkling. She told them that she had answered every question perfectly!

The next day, to celebrate, Papá invited Uncle Luis for supper. Papá even came home from work early to help prepare the meal.

"I need chicken," Mamá said, gathering up her sewing.

Papá stood up to go, but Mamá said, "No, I go."

Ana said, "I'll go too."

At the store, Mamá and Ana stood in line to pay. The clerk rang up the chicken. Once again the price was not right.

"Chicken," said Mamá, pointing to the sign in the back. "On sale!"

Ana grabbed Mamá's hand and squeezed it. Mamá squeezed back.

"Chicken on sale," she repeated, holding tight to her money.

The clerk looked up and noticed the sale sign. After a short pause he turned to Mamá with a slight smile.

"Oh, sorry. You're right," he said and rang up the correct price.

Ana took her mother's hand when they came out of the store.

"You did it!" Ana cheered. She danced around on the sidewalk.

"I did it!" Mamá hugged Ana and swung her around twice.

Ana and Mamá hurried back to the apartment building and opened the heavy front door. On the third floor Papá, Uncle Luis, and the twins were waiting.

"We're here," Ana called up the stairwell.

"Sí," said Mamá. "We're home."